HELLO,
HUGLESS
DOUGLAS!

DAVID MELLING

WELCOME TO THE WORLD OF
HUGLESS DOUGLAS...

Hugless Douglas loves his friends
and he loves hugs, especially best
friend hugs!

This is Rabbit, one of Douglas's
wisest friends.

Watch out for the Funny
Bunnies – they're
bouncing bundles of fun!

The sheep are a crazy,
cuddly, friendly bunch.

A DAY WITH DOUGLAS!

Douglas wakes up
every morning with a
BIG, BIG WAKE-UP HUG.

After a sticky
breakfast…

he gets dressed…

brushes his fur
(and teeth)…

and rushes outside to play.

Douglas soon
bumps into the
Funny Bunnies.

After a **BOUNCY** morning, it's time to find the sheep...

Climbing can be tricky.
But if Douglas has a
problem, he can always
count on his friends.

And they can always
count on him.

At the end of a fun-filled day, it's tea and bathtime

(sometimes together).

Douglas always reads a story before
he goes to sleep. He loves books.

And he loves hugs!
NIGHT, NIGHT,
HUGLESS DOUGLAS.

HUG GALLERY

Balloon hug

Best friend hug

Birthday hug

Big toy hug

Upside-down hug

Woolly hug

Falling hug

Sandwich hug

Pyjamas hug

Blanket hug

World Book Day hug

DAD HUGS FOR MONIKA AND LUKA. D.M.

This book has been specially written and published for World Book Day 2014.
For further information, visit www.worldbookday.com.

World Book Day in the UK and Ireland is made possible
by generous sponsorship from National Book Tokens,
participating publishers, authors and booksellers.

Booksellers who accept the £1 World Book Day Book Token
bear the full cost of redeeming it.

World Book Day, **World Book Night** and **Quick Reads** are annual initiatives
designed to encourage everyone in the UK and Ireland – whatever your age –
to read more and discover the joy of books.

World Book Night is a celebration of books and reading for adults
and teens on 23 April, which sees book gifting and celebrations in
thousands of communities around the country:
www.worldbooknight.org

Quick Reads provides brilliant short new books by
bestselling authors to engage adults in reading:
www.quickreads.org.uk

First published in 2014 by Hodder Children's Books,
a division of Hachette Children's Books, 338 Euston Road,
London NW1 3BH
An Hachette UK Company